Anthony Strickland
Killa City

Ki

FIRST EDITION

www.bellepoetry.com

1

Anthony Strickland
Killa City

Ki

ACKNOWLEDGEMENT

I WANNA FIRST THANK GOD FOR ALLOWING ME THE CHANCE TO LIVE AND SHARE THIS MOMENT WITH YOU.

I WANNA THANK MY WIFE COURTNEY STRICKLAND FOR MOTIVATION AND SUPPORT IN MAKING THIS POSSIBLE. SHE IS ALSO AN AUTHOR OF POETRY AND IS ½ OF THE MOUTH FROM THE SOUTH.

ALSO ANTHONY CRAWFORD JR. A GREAT FRIEND, NOVELIST, AND EDUCATOR WHO NOT ONLY EDITED THIS BOOK BUT TOOK PART IN INSPIRING IT'S RELEASE.

TAVIE THE POET AND POETIC CITY FOR HELPING OUR WORDS TO COME OUT. THE MOVEMENT IS REAL….
SPECIAL APPRECIATION TO DA CREW

> DERR'ION GRAY
> RANDY POWELL
> RODERICK MORRISON
> CHAD HAWKINS
> MARQUES PAYNE
> DOUGLAS HEATH
> ISSAC SKANES
> NICK SMITH
> ROBERT RICHARDSON
> CURTIS WILLIAMS

Anthony Strickland
Killa City

Ki

THIS BOOK IS FICTION BUT LOYALTY IS REAL. THE NAMES I USED ARE ALL MY DAY ONES AND REAL RECOGNIZE REAL. SO I HOPE YALL ENJOY KILLA CITY PART 1 AND TRUST, PART 2 COMING SOON.......

Anthony Strickland
Killa City

Ki

TONY

Ki

"Wake up Nigga!"

That was the first thing I heard. I rolled over to look at the clock and had to blink twice. Damn, there she was! She was standing by the bed naked, water dripping from that sexy brown skin. I laid in the bed speechless, licking my top lip slowly. When I opened my mouth to speak, she silenced me.

"Don't even think about it, Tony," Kesha said as she walked to the closet. "You know I gotta go to class this morning and you got shit to do."

"But Baby, we both got time for a lil' quickie," I said as I pulled her to the bed.

"Boy stop playing," she said as she pushed me back into the bed. "Get up and get ready."

She turned and walked into her closet. I just watched as that ass moved to the beat. She bent over to pick some shoes then turned and caught me looking. I smiled, and she shook it for me one time before she gave me that look. I knew what that look meant.

"Aight Damn!"

I got up and took a quick shower, jumped fresh, and went downstairs. I smelled baby cooking that grown breakfast for a nigga. I

Ki

walked in the kitchen and smacked her on the ass. She loves that shit.

I sat down right before she put that plate in my face. While rubbing my stomach, I asked, "Damn baby, this what good dick get ya huh?" I laughed. It was French toast, bacon, and eggs, with mama biscuits; on point!

"What you want to drink baby," she said.

"I'll take some OJ," I replied as I looked at my watch. "Fuck, we gotta go if we gonna get you to class on time."

"Okay, Daddy," she said while grabbing her purse.

"I love it when you call me that shit girl," I said as I pulled her mouth to mine, kissing and caressing those thick, juicy lips. We had to catch our-damn-selves for a minute. "Go get your books, I'll start the truck."

I walked outside, stretching. The morning air hit me hard. The neighborhood was quiet. Probably because I only had two neighbors. I like it that way; need peace after a good day of making money. At least I thought so anyway.

I walked to the driveway and took a look at my truck. KUSHING. 2018 CADILLAC ESCALADE ON OLD MEN. Every time I see it, I brush my shoulders off.

6

Ki

All black on black on black. Slappin! I'm glad Kesha talked me into buying this truck.

She finally walked up, and I opened the door. She hopped in and handed me her bag. I threw it in the back seat before I got in. I started the truck, turned up the music, fired up, and pulled away from the curb.

We made it to the school in 15 minutes. I parked and looked at Kesha. ***The craziest thought crossed my mind. "Baby why is it you never drive your car to class?"

She sat back and gave me a look and said, "Cause you bought it and knew I didn't want it."

"What you mean? A BMW? Girl you tripping."

She pushed me and said, "No, I'm not. Look around nigga! Everything is simple and boring here. If I drive that car here, they gonna know my man is a drug dealer."

"And how would they know that?" I asked while smiling.

She laughed and answered, "Cause I'm a black bitch getting an A1 education! Plus, I'm the daughter of a kingpin"

We laughed, and I responded, "Girl you crazy."

My phone rang, and it was my nigga Yella calling.

Ki

"What up Gangsta! What you doing up so early?" I asked when I answered the phone.

"What you mean?" He asked while laughing. "Can't get money sleeping like you do BOSS and it's not like we have an easy day. Where you at anyway?"

"I'm dropping Kesha off at class, hold up." I sat the phone on the console. Kesha opened her door, leaned over and gave me a kiss. "Tell Yella I said thank you."

"He said for what baby?"

"Saving me," she said as she closed the door. "I'll see you later baby, I love you and say hey to my daddy for me."

I watched that ass jiggle till it was out of my view then got back to my call. "My bad Yella, what's good?"

"Maintaining mane! We got that meeting with Gripp this morning! Plus, we need to make some runs so come thru and let's get it!"

"Damn, I forgot all about Gripp, that's why you my right-hand man. I'm on my way."

"Cool but Tony, if I had a chick like Kesha, I'll be forgetful too," Yella said while laughing like a fat boy.

"You stupid," I said laughing back. "I'll be there in two shakes of a Lions Tail!"

"Already," he said as we hung up.

Anthony Strickland
Killa City

Ki

      I was on my way to Yella's spot when I saw the blue lights behind me. "What the hell now?" I whispered to myself as I put my blunt in the ashtray and sprayed the car. I knew it was some bullshit, so I pulled over and let down the window.

      "What's going on Tony?" The officer said as he blew cigar smoke in my face.

      I looked at him with a mean mug. "Nothing much," I said waving my hand back and forth, fanning the smoke. "Why you pull me over? Kesha already cooked me bacon this morning."

      "Because I wanted to, BOY! He said while tapping his gun.

      I laughed and thought to myself, "Pussy."

      "Anything in here I need to know about?"

      "Yeah, my licensed 45. Loaded. I said putting it on the dash. Now why you fucking with me?"

      Detective Ode White was a lead dick for the police department and one of my Boss's bitches. Not to mention, he's Kesha's Ex. He's always fucking with me but can't touch me. "Fucking bitch," I whispered to myself.

      "You better watch your mouth Tony," he said while throwing down his cigar. "I don't

Ki

like checking up on you no more than you; just reminding you about Friday with the Boss."

"Today's Thursday, asshole," I said with a smart tone.

"I know you lil' shit! Just letting you know," he said as he walked back to his car. He got in and drove away.

Anthony Strickland
Killa City

Ki

Anthony Strickland
Killa City

Ki

    "One day I'm gonna kill that nigga" I said to myself as I drove off. "Damn, now I'm gonna be late.

    "When I finally got to Yella's crib, he was already standing outside. He hopped in, said "What up Tony!" and closed the door.

    "Not Shit," I said while shaking his hand.

    "What the fuck took you so long?" He asked.

    "Mann," I said irritated. "I got fuck with by White bitch ass again!"

    "Stop playing, Tony, again? Damn folks. If you want, I'll go shoot him in the fucking face G!" Yella said, tapping his chest.

    "Naw," I said while tapping his chest. "Gripp will have our ass if we do. Don't trip though, I can handle White."

    "Aight," Yella said, putting his gun away. "But in case you forgot, you fucking the Boss daughter, don't think he gonna trip too much over a cop. Regardless if it's White or not"

    We laughed hard. I replied "Yeah, you might be right. Let's get to this meeting."

    We were supposed to meet Gripp at his pool hall. We were almost 15 minutes late. When we pulled up, Pain's right hand was standing at the door. "What up Tony. Yella.

Ki

You nigga's late again," Bam said as we all showed love.

"What up Bam," I said. "My bad, bruh! Got held up. We Good?"

"Naw, hell my Boss ain't here either. Guess he knew you were gonna be late," Bam said laughing. "Ya'll wanna smoke one while we wait?"

"Bet," I said pulling out my keys. "I wanna show you my new truck anyway." I hit a button as we walked over. It started, Tutzilla coming out the back.

We walked over and hopped in. Bam looked around and shouted, "Damn Nigga! How many TVs you need in this bitch?"

I laughed and answered, "Shidddd you can never have too many!" I passed him the blunt.

"I feel that," he said as he inhaled. "So, how's the business?"

"Cool," Yella said as he grabbed the blunt. "Except for this one cat who don't know how to follow the rules."

Bam rubbed his chin. "Who's that?" He asked as he set up.

"Nobody," I said calming him down. "I'll handle it."

"Damnnnnn. Now that's a whip Tony." I looked up to see Pain coming into the parking lot.

13

Ki

Pain pulled up, shinning, as usual. He was the underboss of the squad and second in command. Believe me, he for damn sure made his presence known. Four houses, way too many cars, and an army of hood soldiers always around him. Today, he was in an old school, and it was hot. Candy blue with matching inside, Pain wrote all over the car, shits hot.

"What up Pain," I said as we got out the truck. "I'm loving the whip my guy. We know who getting money around here!" We all laughed. He stepped out in all Polo. We met Pain at the door.

Bam, my Nigga showing the *homie* love. "Tony, Yella; what's good with you Fellas? Sorry, I'm late."

"No worries Pimp," I responded as we sat by the window.

Pain looked outside and with tight eyes said, "Loving the truck. What are those 26-inch rims?"

"We just gonna call them Grown," I said as I sipped my drink. "Clean as Fuck huh?"

"Nice my Nigga," he declared. "I had to do it different for the old school though, 25 inches. Just like the Block."

"That shit tight as Fuck," said Yella.

14

Ki

"Thanks Fam," Pain said as they nodded. "C'mon, let's handle business."

"Bet," I concluded as we all walked to the back tables.

"Have a seat, Fellas. Ya'll need another drink?" Pain asked as he grabbed the Crown from behind the bar. Me and Yella both accepted. Bam left to get more glasses. When he got back, we poured and got to business. "So how much you got for me today Tony?" Pain pulled out his money machine and placed it on the counter.

I pulled the bread out the bag. "I got a Lil under $214,000 for you this week."

He looked at me and asked, "Is that All? Why you short this week?"

"Man, I had a lil' problem," I said rubbing my fade. "But it's something I gotta handle on my own. Won't happen again."

Pain sat back. "A Problem?" He said pulling out his nine and looking evil. "What's that?"

"Nothing. I got it under.....".

Pain slapped the table and stood up. "Hold up Tony," he said grabbing my shoulder. "You are one of my best captains. You bring in almost $350,000 a week, and you fucking my sister! But now you over 100 short? So what you want me to tell Gripp, that you had a fucking problem?"

I looked at Pain and said, "I don't want you to tell Gripp shit! I ain't got time for him thinking I can't handle my shit. I got this."

"You sure?" He asked. "Cause I can let Bam handle this shit for you. He ain't shot nobody in a while and his finger needs some exercise."

We all looked at Bam and laughed.

"Real Shit," Bam said pulling out his tech-nine. "I'm ready to murder a Nigga."

"Naw Bam, me and Yella gonna handle this," I said motioning for him to put his gun away. "Pain, my bad for the short but it ain't no thang, I'll handle it."

"I know," Pain said sipping his drink. "We just looking out. How's my sister doing?" He went back to counting.

"She's good. You should call her," I said as I got up from the table.

"I think I will," he said as we shook hands.

"Bet, we out players, see ya'll next Friday night" I said while leaving the pool hall.

As we were getting in the truck, my phone rang. It was Kesha. "What's up baby?" I said.

Ki

"Nothing much boo, on lunch about to go to my next class. I miss you and wanted to see what you were doing…" She said, sexing that voice up.

"Just left from seeing your brother, about to go see a couple of workers and check on my spots. And I miss you too," I added before she snapped.

"That's what's up" she said. "Was my dad there?"

"Naw," I answered. "Just him and Bam and oh yeah, your bitch ass ex fucked with me again this morning after I dropped you off."

"Again?"

"Hell yeah. He starting to piss me off," I said sounding tight.

"Aye Nigga, stop the truck!" Yella said grabbing my arm.

"Baby let me call you back, I gotta handle something. Love ya."

"I love you too baby," she replied. "And I told you about that I!"

I laughed as I hung up. "What's the deal Nigga?" I asked as I pulled over the truck.

Yella grabbed his strap and said, "There's that Bitch Ass Nigga again!" We jumped out the truck. We walked up calmly. "What the fuck you think you doing Nigga?"

"What you think I'm doing Nigga?" Memphis said.

17

Anthony Strickland
Killa City

Ki

"It looks like you trying to set up shop in my shit," I said while mean-mugging him.

"Well we gotta make money too!"

"What?" I said as I looked down at his homeboy. "Who the fuck are you?"

"I'm Tracy," he responded looking stupid.

I laughed and cock my gun. "GO MAKE THAT SHIT SOMEWHERE ELSE NIGGA!" Yella screamed pointing his gun.

"Chill Dog," Memphis said. "We leaving. Let's go yall." Him and his boys started to move, but Tracy stood his ground.

Yella walked up to him, put the barrel between the nigga's eyes, and demanded, "Leave Bitch. Now!" Yella had no hint of playing. Tracy quietly turned and walked with his crew. We watched them for a second then got back in the truck.

I lit a Newport and looked at Yella. "You know we gonna have to kill them Niggas right?" I said inhaling.

"I know," Yella said. "The streets watching." Suddenly, his phone rang. "What up Smurf?" He said while answering the phone. He spoke for a second or two then hung up. "That was Young Smurf ready for some keys." Yella took out his extended clip.

"Fuck them niggas, we got shit to do. Let's get back to work."

19

After we made all the drop offs and met with the squad, I got a text from Kesha telling me she was already at home. I drove to Yella's spot to drop him off before I headed home for the day.

When I got home, I seen Bam's 300 parked in front of my crib. I pulled in the driveway and parked. By the time I grab my things Bam was already opening my door.

"What up Bam?"

"What's good Tony," he replied helping me with my shit. "Just came by to let you know that it's some frails in our mists."

"What?" I said with a surprise look. "Who?"

"We don't know yet," he said as we walked to the door. "White supposed to let us know at the meeting tomorrow."

"FUCK!" I yelled furiously. "If it ain't one thing it's another. Thanks G. You could have called me with this though, why you drive way out here to my spot?"

Man, I had to pick Yetta up from school and she wanted to see Kesha's 'New House'," he said with a laugh. "So, I just brought her home."

"You like the house, Bam?"

"Yeah," he answered looking around. "Just too much damn grass. Who gonna cut this shit?"

"Pedro," I said as we both shared a good laugh and went into the house.

When we got in the house; Yetta already had on her coat. She walked over and gave me a big hug then looked at Bam and asked, "Are you ready to go?"

I looked at him. "Leaving already?" I asked, sounding surprised. "You just got here."

"Naw Nigga," she said laughing. "You just got here. Shit we been here for hours." She picked up her backpack. "Plus, I got homework."

"Aight sis," I said as I hugged her.

She looked at Bam and said, "C'mon" snappy as hell. I laughed.

"Aight Damn," he said. "Why you rushing anyway?"

"Yall crazy," I said as I closed the door, laughing. I locked it then walked through the house. "KESHA? WHERE YOU AT BABY?" I yelled through the crib. "I'm hungry!"

"I'm upstairs!" She yelled. "Come up here."

"Damn," I thought to myself. "It better be some food up there."

21

Ki

"I'm coming," I yelled and started walking towards the stairs. As I walked upstairs, I smelled peaches. "I must be really hungry," I thought.

I walked in the bedroom to see Kesha lying on the bed with a bowl of peaches sitting on her naked body. Her nipples were hard as a rock and I could tell that she wanted me in many ways.

"Hey baby," she said as she lit a blunt.

"Hey sexy," I said still staring. "What you doing?"

"Waiting on you to get home so you could Cum and Smoke with me," she said as she hit the blunt. "What took you so long?"

"Yella had to check on his ride. Peaches huh?" I said licking my lips.

"Yes Daddy," she said smiling. "After a long day you need your nutrients."

"You're right about that baby," I said excitedly. "And you know I can eat a peach for hours."

She smiled and responded, "Well, why don't you start with this one?" She put the blunt in the ashtray, she turned and laid flat on her back, and then opened her legs. That fat pussy was waiting to be tasted.

I walked over and started kissing her. I grabbed her plump ass, kissed her cheek, then I smacked it with light force. She moaned so seductive that my dick jumped out my boxers. I moved down and started slowly licking that pussy just the way she liked it.

She couldn't control herself. She started making them moaning sounds. I licked my finger and put it inside of her. She instantly grabbed my head and pushed me deeper, so I can catch all her cum.

"Oh Daddy," she moaned. "I want you inside me."

I looked at her shaking my head. "Naw baby," I said. "You know I like teasing you." I took a slice of the peaches and rubbed it on her clit very slowly. She tried her best to hold it in, so I went faster. After about 30 seconds, she was squirting all over the bed. I got up and burped as I wiped off my mouth, smiling.

"Oh yeah," she said, throwing a pillow. "You think that's funny?"

"Come on baby," I said. "You know I love to watch you cum."

"Oh yeah?" She said as she grabbed my arm. She laid me on the bed and put her lips to mine. She pushed her tongue deep inside my mouth and took control. She pulled back and asked, "You think you can tease me huh?"

"Oh shit," I thought to myself. She grabbed my dick and put me inside her. She started grinding slow and lovely, allowing my

Anthony Strickland
Killa City

Ki

dick to go in deep and slow. She moaned then
jumped up and ran out the room.

"What the Fuck?" I said as I sat up.

She stood at the door, smiling, then said,
"You gotta come and get it." She ran
downstairs, laughing. I got up and ran after her
while her juices were still dripping from my
dick.

I walked down the stairs but didn't see
her. "Why is she playing with me," I said to
myself. I walked into the living room towards
the couch. "OH SHIT!" I said startled. She
jumped from behind the curtain and threw me
against the wall. She kissed my back as she
started playing with my dick. I was throbbing in
her hand. She turned me around and licked my
nipples hard.

She slowly went down and started
sucking my dick, slow and short. "Damn baby!"
I said as I put my arms in the air. "That shit
feels so damn good."

She stopped and looked up at me,
grinning. "I know," she said.

By that time, I was rock hard. I reached
down, grabbed her by her cheeks, and picked
her up. Slowly, I put my dick inside her lips and
we made passionate love.

Two hours later, we both lay on the
floor trying not to pass out. "I love you Tony,"
she said kissing my chest.

Anthony Strickland
Killa City

Ki

Ki

"I love you too girl," I replied as I kissed her on the forehead. We both passed out on the floor.

Bam looked at his watch. "It's 11:19pm," he said. "I'm hungry Yetta. You gonna cook or are we gonna go grab something?"

She looked at him with a smirk and replied, "I'm not cooking anything tonight. Go to Rudy's." He knew she was going to say that, so he was already in route.

Bam pulled in the drive thru of Rudy's and noticed a car following them. Yetta noticed it, too. "Who is that baby?" She asked scarcely.

"I don't know," Bam said as he reached for his gun. He cocked it and sat it on his lap. He pulled forward to order.

As he ordered the food, Bam kept his eye on the car behind him. Yetta reached down to get her phone and said, "I'm gonna call Tony! I got a bad feeling."

"What?" Bam said grabbing the phone. "Don't call Tony, this might not be shit. Let's just get the food and get home."

As he said that, Yetta screamed. Bam turned around to a glock pointed at his face.

"GET YOUR BITCH ASS OUT THE CAR," Manny demanded as he grabbed Bam's gun.

26

Ki

As Bam got out the car, he noticed the
guys who Yella and Tony had to check earlier
that day.

"What the fuck ya'll want?" He said
angry as hell.

"Calm down Bam," Manny said. "We
just got a message for your man's."

"My man's?" Bam said looking
confused. "Who's that?"

"That nigga Tony. That is his sister you
fucking right?"

"Fuck you Bitch," Bam said unfolding
his arms.

"Watch your fucking mouth."

As Bam finished his sentence, Tracy
came up and tried to hit Bam from the back.
Yetta jumped out the car pointing her 25 and
screaming, "DON'T YOU TOUCH HIM..."

"WHAT?" Tracy said. "What the fuck
you gonna do with that lil ass pistol,
Bitch?"

Bam swung and punch Tracy in the
mouth breaking his jaw. He fell to the
ground.

Manny cocked his shot gun, and
everyone got quiet. He walked up to Bam.
"Look Nigga," he said staring in Bam's eyes.
"We really don't have time for this bullshit.
Yetta, that's your name, right?"

27

Ki

"Fuck you," she said.

"Spunky. I like that," Manny said, smiling. "Tell your brother his blocks now belong to me."

"What? Nigga you done lost your damn mind," Bam said with anger. "Do you think Tony gonna let this shit ride? You think he gonna take this shit from you? Your ass will be dead before you collect from our blocks."

"Naw Bam," Manny said shaking his head. He told his crew to pick up Tracy and they got in the car and drove off.

Bam looked at Yetta and ask her if she was alright. She nodded. They got in the car and he gave her back her phone. "I guess you can make that call," he said with his head down.

"What is it Bam?" She asked.

He looked at her and said, "We got one problem though."

"What?" She asked, putting on her seatbelt.

Bam rubbed his fade and calmly said, "Them frails are cops."

"Damn…." She said dropping her head.

"Fuck it," Bam said. "Let's go home and deal with this shit in the morning."

"OK," she said, and they drove home.

The next morning, the whole crew met up at Gripp's club. The whole squad, including me who runs the East, Nine Milli who runs the West, Doug D who runs the North, and Skanes who runs the South. Pain is second in command and Gripp controls the state. Every right-hand man was there as well.

"Money!" Gripp said and everyone repeated. "How ya'll doing?"

"Sleepy," Nine Milli answered. "Why we meeting so early anyway?"

"First off," Gripp said calmly. "Cause I said so." We all laughed. "Secondly, seems we have a problem that needs to be tended to."

"Problem?" Doug D said loudly. "What problem?" Doug D was a fighter from Texas who has a habit of breaking jaws.

Pain then stood and addressed the group. "Fellas, last night my nigga, Bam, got a gun put in his face by three niggas who wanted to deliver a message."

I jumped up fast and tight as hell. "Bam! With my sister in the fucking car?! Why the fuck you didn't call me?!"

"Because Gripp told me not to," Bam said looking at the Boss.

"What the fuck Gripp?" I said looking at my boss. "Why?"

"Sit down lil' nigga," Gripp said lightly. "It's because the niggas are cops, plus no one got hurt."

29

Ki

"Cops?" I said sitting down. "What was the fucking message?"

"That they taking over, Tony," Bam said playfully. "And they starting with you."

I jumped up and professed, "What? Why would they attempt to do some stupid shit like that? And why not start with Skanes? He is the easiest to get." The whole room started laughing.

Skanes looked around. "Ya'll tripping," he said. "My people hate problems and love exercise. Try if you want." He laughed.

"Nigga mine either," I said and then looked at Bam. "So, Bam, you got a plan or what? You know who they are?"

He sipped his drink before he answered, "Memphis, Tracy, and Manny." Yella jumped up and punched the table while I sat back rubbing my fade.

"What the Fuck is it?" Gripp asked, quieting the whole room.

Yella spoke before I did, "We ran into them niggas yesterday and ran them off the Block. Knew I should've killed that bitch." He took a sip of his drink. "What's the move?" He pulled out his glock.

"I got White on it. He gonna figure out where these frails came from. But if you see them in your shit again, shoot they ass in the fucking nose." Everybody fell out laughing.

Ki

"In the nose Gripp?" I said laughing.

He smiled, opened his safe, and asked, "What the Fuck I say?" He laughed as he reached in the safe and pulled out a box of envelopes. He passed them out one by one. After he was done, he sat at the table and made him a cup. "This here is a bonus for ya'll ass. Bee loves her new car from the last quarter." He looked at his right-hand Doe and held up his pinky.

Doe got up to address us. "Aye, ya'll Niggas having fun?" We all nodded. "Good, now get the fuck out. Don't spend all that shit in one place ya dig." He had that look on his face.

One thing about Doe, nigga was born rich. Had everything he wanted, including the best guns around. He met Gripp when he was 16 on a holiday in T-Town. Gripp was having words with the connect when Doe walked in and shot him in the ass. Gripp looked at Doe and since kept him close. We never knew why Doe shot that nigga. We just knew to stay on his good side.

We all got up and started making our way to the parking lot. Gripp came to the door and said, "I'll see ya'll niggas tonight." That was the last thing he said before he closed the door.

Ki

Nine Milli looked at us and said, "What the fuck? Why Doe kick us out like that?"

"Nigga you ain't know?" Doug D asked loudly. "When Gripp dismiss you, he dismiss you. Who the fuck gonna say a word after Doe speak."

We all laughed. Me and Yella showed love to the fellas then hopped in Yella's whip. "Damn, I'm hungry," I told him as he started the car.

He rubbed his belly and replied, "Shidddd, me to. Let's go to Roscoe's." We left and made our way through the streets of Oklahoma City on a nice breezy day.

It was almost 9:30 by the time we hit the parking lot. We got out and went in. We sat at Roscoe's looking at the menu and drinking coffee. We both ordered and gave back our menus. I pulled out my envelope and opened it. "Damn," I said counting the Benjamin's. "That nigga Gripp be giving nice tax-free bonuses." I smiled hard at the new money.

"They feel better in ya hands. How much you got there Tony?" Yella asked pulling out his envelope.

"Shit, to be honest, it looks like 57,000. What about you?" I asked while putting mine back in the envelope.

Anthony Strickland
Killa City

Ki

NINE MILLI

"Man its 54,000," he answered, smiling. "Shit, thank you Gripp." He put the money back in his pockets.

"Really Yella?" I said shaking my head. "You gonna walk around with 54 racks in your pocket?"

He looked at me and laughed. "With my Glock in my waist. Today ain't the day for forgiveness."

Our food arrived. Before eating, we thanked God for the meal. As we said amen, we looked up to a couple starring at us. Yella looked at them and said, "Thugs need Jesus too. Probably more than you." We all laughed the tension away.

After we finished our meal, we hit the streets to holla at the crew. We met up with Doug D at the car wash.

"What up D," I said as we got out the car.

"What up players. What ya'll on?"

"Shit," I said. "Trying to see how we gonna handle this nigga Manny. D passed the blunt."

"Hell," he said. "On site. I ain't playing no games. I'm about to have a baby which means I don't play with other people kids bruh. For real, For real."

Ki

Skanes pulled up and hopped out. As he did, so did Nine Milli. They walked over and we all chopped it up while the whips were being cleaned. After they got ready, we all shook hands and went outside.

As me and Yella were getting in the car, Pain pulled up with three bad bitches in his ride, bumping Jay Z and Alicia Keys. He opened the door to the Benz and got out.

"Boss man," I said as I shook his hand. "What's good?"

"Not Shit," he replied opening the back door. "Bout to get some food while the whip gets a bath."

"That's what's up," Yella said, eyeing the ladies that were getting out. "Keep the condom tight Boss man. We gotta make some runs."

He smiled like a proud father. "Now that's what I like to hear," he said walking to the other side of the car. He opened the other doors. "What's the standing around for? Ya'll get at it."

We showed love, walked away, got in the car, and rode out.

I sat at my main spot counting money when my phone rang. It was Gripp. "What up Gripp?" I said when I answered.

Anthony Strickland
Killa City

Ki

"What up Tony. So that Frail White hit me back with some info on Manny and his Crew."

"Oh yeah. What's poppin?"

"Well," he said after a pause. "Tracy and Manny are Frails. The other one, Memphis, is not. He just started in the game and he figure taking me down is a good way to get a name for himself. Fucking dumbasses!"

"Don't he know who the fuck you are? This has been tried before?"

Gripp got quiet. He answered, "Yeah. He knows exactly who I am. When I took over Kansas, it belonged to his bitch ass daddy. Guess he want it back." He laughed and concluded, "But he needs to see Lil' Linc. Hell, I gave him control when he got out."

"Damn," I said shaking my head. "So how you wanna handle this seriously."

Gripp cleared his throat. "Simple," he said. "Turns out he on they radar. It's only a matter of time before it catches up but it the meantime, it's a green light. I'm gonna hit Lil' Linc today and put him up on game."

"Nough said Boss. I got you. Gone."
We hung up. I thought about what Gripp said as I finished counting money. I hit Yella up to let him know the deal. I packed the safe, locked up the spot, and left to get Kesha from school.

Anthony Strickland
Killa City

Ki

On my way to pick up Kesha, I spotted Pain at Tate's Rim Shop. I pulled over to holla at him. "What's good My Nigga?" I said as I got out the truck.

"Shit," he replied while shaking my hand. "Caught a flat on my box Chevy so I figure why not put some new rims on her as well."

"Damn Pain, you just got them a few months ago. Balling Ass!"

We laughed. "You know I gotta look rich as fuck! But they tripping!" He said while looking at the salesman. "Yo, what's the fucking holdup?" The salesman looked at him nervously. "Nigga must not know who the Fuck I am."

The salesman hit the register and said, "$4,700 please sir."

Pain yelled, "Just put it on my tab!"

The salesman rubbed his head and said, "I need to see your ID before I can put it on an account."

Pain turned and starred at the salesman hard. "What the fuck you say to me?" He asked while reaching. "Boy you about to get...."

I grabbed his shoulder before he finished. "I got this boss." I pulled $5,000 out my pocket and gave it to the salesman.

Anthony Strickland
Killa City

Ki

Ki

Pain looked at me then back the salesman. "Say thank you," he said. "This nigga just saved your life." Pain grabbed his keys and we both walked out the shop. "Why you save him Tony?"

As he opened his door, I answered, "Cause boss, I gotta pick up Kesha. Plus, that was cheaper than your bail would have been." We laughed, shook hands, and went our separate ways.

When I made it to the school, Kesha and Yetta were standing outside, talking by a building. I had Tutzilla playing so my sounds were banging. They both started dancing and popping. I watched them and laughed as I recorded them for a snapchat story.

They both hopped in the truck. "Hey baby," Kesha said as she leaned over to kiss me. I kissed her back.

"What's up baby? How was your day?"

"It was good," she responded, putting on her seatbelt.

"What's up Yetta. You good?"

"Yeah Bro, I'm straight.," she said, looking around. "Where the weed at?"

I looked at her and laughed. The fact that my sister smoke is still a surprise to me. I handed her a blunt. "Why didn't you call me

Ki

last night after that bullshit happen Yetta? You
know I don't play that shit," I said while driving
off.

"You forget who my man is?" she asked
with a smirk.

Bam said, "Don't call," so I didn't. I
stopped a red light.

"Listen sis, I don't care who you
fucking, I'm your protection and don't you
forget that again." She sat back and frowned up.
"Do you understand Yetta?"

"Yeah," she said with an attitude. "I
hear you."

Kesha touch my arm and I told her,
"You should have called but sometimes you
gotta respect what your nigga says."

"Shut up!" Yetta screamed from the
back seat. "Your ass wouldn't have called either
if Tony told you not to. Family or not. Stop
acting."

I cleared my throat and said, "Both of
ya'll chill out, it's good but it better not happen
again."

"Whatever," Yetta said hitting the blunt.

The light turned green and we headed
towards the crib. I made a stop at the liquor
store to buy a bottle of D'usse. "Ya'll want
anything?" I asked as I got out the truck.

They both said "Naw" and I walked in
the store.

Anthony Strickland
Killa City

Ki

"Girl, I can't wait to get to the club tonight," Yetta said excited.

"Me too," Kesha said playing on her phone. "After this long ass week, we all need to relax. What you gonna wear?"

"IDK," Yetta said while thinking. "Something tight."

They both laughed as the door to the truck swung open. Memphis yanked Kesha out of the truck. Yetta started screaming as she reached for her gun.

While I'm in the store paying for my drink, I heard a scream coming from outside. I instantly ran out the store cocking my glock as I hit the parking lot. I pointed my gun directly at his head. "Take your fucking hands off my girl." I said as calmly as I could.

"Awww Tony mad," Memphis said laughing. "We always meeting with guns

Anthony Strickland
Killa City

Ki

YETTA

between us. Put it down lil boy." Memphis smiled.

"Fuck you," I said, gripping my gun. "Not till you let her go."

"Look Tony. Ya'll fighting a battle ya'll can't win. Don't make this hard lil guy."

"You think so," I said smiling. "Nigga why you think they call this the Killa City? It ain't just me you fucking with faggot!"

Memphis laughed and said, "Boy I know exactly who we fucking with. You don't know who the fuck I am?"

I looked at him closely. "I don't give a fuck who you are or what you about."

"Wrong answer nigga," Memphis said.

I don't think he knew those would be his last words. Soon as he finished his sentence, a bullet went through his skull. His limped body fell to the ground. I watched it fall. I looked up and Yetta was standing with her gun smoking, looking like she was about to cry. Kesha fell to her knees. I reached and picked her up then turned to Yetta.

"Give me the gun sis." Her hands were shaking, and I could tell she was scared as hell. She handed me the gun and turned to look at Memphis's lifeless body.

She spit on him and asked, "That's what I do with that lil' ass pistol!"

43

Ki

I looked but didn't even ask. We walked back to the truck and sped away towards the crib. I grabbed my cell and called Gripp. He answered on the second ring.

"What's up Tony," he said when he answered. I paused. "What nigga?" he said, getting irritated.

"We had to kill that nigga at the store, Boss."

"What!?" Gripp said, jumping out his chair. "What Nigga?"

"That asshole, Memphis."

"WHAT THE FUCK!?" Gripp said, pissed. "Who the fuck was with you?"

"Me, Kesha, and Yetta."

When I said that Gripp got angry as hell. "You mean to tell me that you shot someone while my fucking daughter was in the car?" Before I answered he continued. "Bring ya'll ass to the pool hall NOW!"

He said with a command and hung up. Yetta was still sobbing in the back seat. I turned around to comfort my sister. "Yetta, wipe them tears away," I told her. "By any means necessary, right? Rather eat dinner than be dinner ya dig?" She smiled and seemed to be feeling better.

We headed to the pool hall. By the time we were a block from the pool hall, we heard sirens. We pulled up and saw Pain and Bam standing outside the pool hall. Bam grabbed Yetta and hugged her tightly. Pain grabbed Kesha.

Hugging her he looked at me. "What the fuck happened?" He asked, trying to hold his attitude in.

"G check this." So, I ran down the story to them. When they heard who pulled the trigger, Bam held Yetta tighter all while telling her not to worry.

"Well shit, I guess everyone good. Let's go. Gripp is inside waiting," Pain said.

We all turned and walked in the pool hall. We met Doe at the door. "Take the girls in the office G." He nodded, and they walked away.

Before they got far, Kesha turn and ran to my arms and kissed me deep. "I love you," she said when we could finally breath.

"I love you too," I said. I smacked her ass and she ran off. We went to meet Gripp.

Gripp spoke fast, "Tony, I understand you did what you had to do, and I know you gonna stay 100 if this falls back. But now you have pissed off these greedy ass cops and they coming. I want everybody home now, nobody makes a move." He was about to wave his pinky till he seen Doe wasn't in the room. "Fuck it," he said laughing. "Leave Me." We all got up and moved towards the door. "Tony,"

45

Ki

Gripp yelled at me. "Kesha and Yetta going to
my house tonight." I looked at him but didn't
fight his order.

I went and got in the truck. Blocc Breed
was bumping through the speakers. I drove off
and headed towards the crib. I had made it
almost three blocks before I seen the lights.
"Fuck!" I said. "This is one day I wish this was
White." Manny and Tracy walked to the truck
and before I could say anything, they dragged
me out and arrested me.

They sat me in an interview room for
almost two hours before then came in. Manny
spoke first. "How's it going, Tony? I see you're
comfortable. Now before you speak, let me ask
do you know what this is?"

I looked at the package on the table. I
laughed, "Naw but I'm quite sure your gonna
tell me. Matter fact, why the fuck am I here?
What's the charge?"

Manny smirked, "You're being charged
with the murder of Terrell Jones aka Memphis."

He paused to see my reaction. I didn't
give one. "Murder?!" I said surprised. "What
evidence do you have for that charge?"

Tracy laughed, "We have an eye witness
that saw you pull the trigger. We'll let you
ponder that while we wait for your lawyer."

They got up and started walking out. I said, "How your jaw feel, Detective?"

He tried to rush the table, but Manny stopped him. "Have it your way Tony. But you' going down for this one way or another. No one can help you out this shit boy."

I laughed, "You don't know my lawyer," I said as I lit a Newport, watching them walk out the room.

I called my lawyer. The Mann Law Office's Secretary answered, "The Mann Law Office, this is Lucy speaking, how may I help you?"

I said, "I need to speak with Matt Mann please."

"Sure," she said. "May I ask who's calling?"

"Yes, this is Tony Waters."

"OK." she responded. "Please hold on for a second, Mr. Waters."

A few seconds later, Matt answered, "So you're looking for a Mann baby?"

I laughed. "Matt, this is Tony Waters. I'm in Oklahoma County being charged with murder."

He laughed and asked, "You're kidding, right? You're Downtown?"

"Yeah," I answered fast. "And I haven't called Gripp yet."

"It's cool, Tony," he said. "I'm on my way. I'll have you out in a bit." He hung up. Matt grabbed his keys, coat, and phone and headed out of the office. He hopped in his Acura Legend and pulled out his phone to call Gripp. After filling the Boss in, he headed to the station.

By the time he made it to the station, Kesha was already there. "Hey Kesha," he said smiling. "How are you?"

"I'm OK," she answered. "Be a lot better once you get my man out of here."

"I know," he said grabbing her hand. "Let's go handle that now." They walked into the station. After sitting Kesha at a desk, Matt went into the interview room to talk to Tony. The cops tried to follow, but Matt slammed the door in their face. They talked for almost 30 minutes.

Matt walked out to see the cops talking to the witness. He walked over to Manny and said, "Since your witness is here, we should do a line up and get this mess over with." Manny looked at Tracy and they agreed. Matt irately insisted, "Can we move this along please?"

Manny stood up and said, "This shouldn't take but a second."

Matt looked stunned. "A Second?" He said. "My client has been sitting in there on bullshit charges with no evidence against him. Why don't we drop this shit and we all go home?"

Tracy stood and declared, "Calm down before I make you calm. Soon as our witness comes out the bathroom, we will be ready to do this line up. In the meantime, we will get everything ready. Go sit down!"

Matt laughed, said, "Whatever asshole," and went to the coke machine. He got his soda and walked back to the desk. "You all have ten minutes!"

Ki

While Kesha was sitting at the desk, she saw the girl talking to Manny as he escorted her to the restroom. Once Manny walked off, she got up and walked into the restroom as well.

She checked the stalls to make sure they were empty then pulled out her 22. She waited till the girl came out the stall then quickly pushed the gun into her stomach.

"What the hell?" Rita, the witness, asked surprisingly.

Kesha quickly reacted, "Shut up Bitch!" She cocked her gun before asking, "Do you know who I am? Do you know who I represent?" Rita stood quietly but shook her head. "Good. Then you know Gripp don't like talkers. So, he has a message for you."

Rita was still quiet. She nervously spoke, "What message could Gripp possibly have for me?"

"Keep your damn mouth shut before you make him mad. When you go in this room you better be real stupid. You better not point out Tony." Rita looked surprised and then she tried to speak again until Kesha slapped her face. She looked in her eyes. "Your life ain't worth a fuck to me, but his is." She put her gun away, fixed her hair, and then walked out the bathroom while Rita was still standing still.

As Rita walked in to view the line-up, Tracy smiled. He had paid Rita to point out

Anthony Strickland
Killa City

Ki

Ki

Tony. He closed the door behind him. The light came on and five black men stood behind the glass.

"Ms. Watson, do you see the man who did the shooting tonight?" Manny asked.

Rita looked at the men for a moment then she quickly looked from Kesha to Tracy. She took a deep breath and said, "I don't see him."

Tracy jumped in and firmly asked, "Are you sure? Look again!" He moved her closer to the glass.

"Again sir, he is not there."

Matt looked at Tracy, grabbed his pack, and said, "I'm going to go take a smoke while you release him." He walked out.

An hour later, Tony walked out of the station. He was heated. He met Matt and Kesha at her car. I shook Matt's hand and praised, "You the fucking man G!"

"That's why you pay me the big bucks," he replied, smiling back. They all got in their cars and went their separate ways.

We rode home to slow jams playing in our ears. "So daddy," Kesha said. "You still wanna go to the club tonight?"

I looked at her. "After all this bullshit today, fuck yeah!" We went home and got fresh.

Ki

When we finally made it to the club, it was already lit. The line was around the corner. Me and Kesha got out the truck and walked inside. We went straight to VIP. The room was packed because of an All-Star cast.

Gripp was pouring up a glass for a toast. He raised his glass and we all did the same. "Top of the world niggas," Gripp said as he took a sip. "Raise your glasses, to making money and taking care of family. Salute!"

The whole room said "Salute" and drank their glasses.

Gripp and Pain were standing by the stairs. Pain looked at his dad and ask, "How does it feel to be untouchable, Gripp?"

Gripp smiled at his Son and said, "It feels like the life of a Gangsta."

We hit the dance floor, hard; sweating like we had been dancing all night. Everyone had blunts and cigars in the air, having a good time. If you didn't smoke, you were high just from being in the room.

I looked at Pain. "Where you get this bud from G?" I asked while hitting the Kush.

He smiled and answered, "I got that from da homie, Half Ton. He brought some good shit from California."

"Damn," I said looking at the blunt. "This shit tastes good as hell. Look like I should just eat the bud." We both laughed while

Ki

I rolled another blunt. "I hope you got some more of this shit G."

He smiled and responded, "Hell yeah, I got plenty my guy. Smoke whatever G."

I looked at him and smiled. I said, "That's what's up."

He stopped and said 12 back and we showed love. "You gonna take Gripp a blunt or two?" He asked motioning for his ladies.

"Naw, remember Gripp only smoke on special occasions."

"Oh yeah! I forgot," he said while starring at the ladies at the bar. He looked at me and laughed. "You wanna have some fun?"

I looked at him, shaking my head; I knew he was up to some shit. "We already having fun, what can be better?" I asked wondering.

Bam walked up to us with another bottle. "What's good ya'll?"

"What up Bam," we both said.

"You just in time to get in on this bet," Pain said pulling out some money.

"What bet?" I asked reaching in my pocket as well. "What we betting on?"

He laughed and explained, "Ya'll see them three chicks sitting at the bar?" We both looked down to see three bad bitches looking like stars. They were chocolate, thick, and very nice.

Ki

"OK, so it's bad bitches in the club," I said lighting a blunt. "What about them?"

"Shidddd I bet 2,500 lil mama with the braids suck the best dick." We laughed.

"Pain you tripping, everyone knows it's always the thickest one who sucks dick the best. I'll take your money."

Bam jumped in fast, and said, "Ya'll both tripping. That lil skinny will swallow it whole!" while pulling out his money. "Let me get in on this shit."

Then it was on. I went and told Kesha what was up. One, because I can, and, two, because she's crazy.

Once she finished hearing the story, she laughed and said, "You better win that money then. Matter fact we might step in too."

I looked at her and smiled. So glad my girl knows what it is. I left her and went to the dance floor with the fellas.

We told Doe to get the ladies and send them to one of the private rooms. He shook his head and walked off. We went to the bar and grabbed a few more bottles before we went to the room. We stepped in to the room and sat on the sectional and poured drinks. Bam passed us all blunts, and we fired up.

We were sitting back listening to the music when the door opened. Doe walked in with the ladies. We looked at them for a few seconds then looked at Doe. "Ya Dig," he said, smiling as he closed the door.

Pain got up, walked over the ladies, and said a few words. They all giggled as he was pouring them drinks. After a few seconds, they all came back to the couch and sat down. "Yo, this is Dawn, Moet, and Apple," he said, introducing the ladies. "These are my guys, Tony and Bam. We spoke and continued the party.

After about 30 minutes things started to get heated. I sat back and pulled Dawn back with me. I whispered in her ear and told her she was sexy as fuck. She smiled and started kissing my neck. I was about to say something, but she put her finger over my lips.

"Shhhhh," she said, sounding so sexy, and I did as she commanded.

She slowly moved her hands around the front of my body while kissing spots on my neck. She rose up my shirt and grabbed my nipples using her nails to squeeze tight. Shit felt good. I closed my eyes. She continued.

She unbuckled my belt and pants with one hand. Damn, she got skills. She reached her hand inside my pants and grabbed my dick. Squeezing and pumping the blood alive in me. She went down and kiss the tip and I jumped.

Damn her lips felt good on my dick. She jacked it off while she kissed me from my

Ki

stomach to my nipples. She suck my nipples
hard then soft. That shit turned me on. After
sucking both my nipples and feeling my dick
get rock hard in her hand, she went back down.

She started with the tip then went deep.
Her mouth was warm and wet. She slowly came
back up making slurping noises. Then she
increased her speed, bobbing her head up and
down to the beat of the music.

When I opened my eyes, all the ladies
were bobbing their heads. I turned to the door
to see Kesha and Yetta standing there. Yetta
had her eyes closed, but Kesha was into it.
Kesha told Yetta to go get her a drink. She
looked and laughed, then walked away. She
then put her attention back to me. She pulled
her skirt up above her waist and slid her thong
to the side. She licked her finger and started
playing with her clit. She motioned her other
hand up and down.

I smiled and grabbed Dawn by her head
and used it like an Xbox joystick. She was
making lovely sounds as her wet mouth went to
work. I looked back at Kesha and she was
rubbing the shit out of her clit. Pussy so good I
could smell it from across the room.

Kesha stopped and pulled down her
skirt as Yetta walked back up with the drinks.
"Bitch you so nasty," she said as she handed
her the drink.

Ki

"Girl, you ain't seen nothing yet," she said as she turned to walk in the room.

Pain jumped when she walked in like she was the police. Me and Bam laughed our ass off. She held up her hand. "Calm down Pain," she said comically. "I'm enjoying the show; I just need to borrow a few of your actors for a sec." She reached down and grabbed Dawn hand and then kissed her on the lips.

"So, what's up, you wanna come home with me and finish this show?" Kesha asked, gripping her ass. Dawn turned and looked at me smiling. She reached down and grabbed my hand and pulled me up. Kesha put my dick back in my pants and zipped me up.

I looked at Bam and Pain. "Well Fellas, the Boss has spoken," I said looking at Kesha. "Guess it's time for us to ride out." I grabbed Kesha and Dawn by the hand and we started walking towards the door.

Before I could open it, Pain called my name. I turned around. "Hold up G," he said as he got up and zipped his pants. He reached in his pocket and handed me $5,000. "That's for that issue." I laughed, and we turned to leave.

We walked by Yetta shaking her head with a smile on her face. She hugged Kesha then turned to me. "Ya'll some nasty people," she said laughing.

Anthony Strickland
Killa City

Ki

 I hugged my sister and told her to go get her man before he fucks up in that room. We looked at Bam and he was in another world.

 "Naw," Yetta said as she looked at her man receiving pleasure from another woman. "I'll wait till he cum. Shit is kinda hot. Bye ya'll," she said as she went into the room and closed the door.

 We said our goodbyes as we headed to the exit. Gripp was waiting for us at the door. He hugged Kesha and showed me some love. "G careful," he said as we walked out to the truck.

 I opened the doors for the ladies. Kesha looked at me smiling. "Time for my fun," she said as she hopped in the back seat with Dawn.

 I laughed and closed the door. I started the truck. Usher started playing as I drove out the parking lot. I almost had a wreck as I looked in my rear-view mirror. Kesha and Dawn were going at it in the back seat. Nights like this I wish I had a Lyft driver. Dawn positioned herself, so Kesha could sit on her face. I grabbed my dick and watched them as I drove through the streets. The moans made me speed up.

 By the time I pulled in the driveway, my whole truck smelled like pussy and peaches. I looked at them and asked if they were ready to go in the house. Dawn pulled her face from in between Kesha's legs, juices dripping from her lips. She looked at Kesha then they both sat up and grabbed their shoes. We all got out the truck and headed inside the house.

When we got into the house, Kesha looked at me. "Go to the bedroom. We will be there in a few," she said, grabbing Dawn hand as they walked away. I shook my head and walked upstairs. I went into the room and put my wallet and gun by the bed. I went to the safe and put my money in there and made sure it was locked.

I took off my shirt and sat on the bed. When I turned to get the remote, Kesha and Dawn walked in wearing nothing. I mean nothing. My dick instantly got hard. I sat back.

Kesha lit a blunt and hit it hard. She passed it to Dawn who hit it hard as well. They both walked towards the bed slow. Kesha got the blunt and hit it again then passed it to me. "Here baby," she said with that sexy ass voice. "Why don't you hit this blunt, while I fuck you. And her."

I looked at Kesha and whispered, "Thank you." She smiled. Her and Dawn went to work while I hit the weed. I guess they had enough of each other for a minute because they both attacked me hard. Stroking and sucking my dick like it was their last meal. Kesha came up and started playing with my nipples while Dawn made my dick hard as a mountain.

Kesha took the blunt from me and begin to hit it as she stood over my face ready to take her seat. She turned to Dawn, and she followed suit ready to drive this stick shift. Kesha hit the blunt again then they started squatting slowly down putting pussy in its place.

Kesha grinding on my face, fucking the shit out of my tongue while Dawn is riding my dick like a horse. They filled the room with moaning and cumming. I felt like I was in heaven.

We switched positions. I bent them both over on the bed. Kesha turned around and smiled at me as I looked at that nice ass in front of me. I walked up to Kesha and slapped her on the ass then shoved plenty of dick deep inside her.

I grabbed Dawn's ass and cuffed it like a basketball then put my thumb in her ass. She moaned loud as she squirted on the bed. As she did, Kesha made the bed wet as well.

Dawn got up and sat in front of Kesha and opened her legs. Kesha grabbed her thighs and pulled her close and licked her while I tore up pussy up from the back. My dick jumped at the sexy sight in front of me.

Kesha came again and fell on the bed. Dawn looked at me and told me to lay down. I

Ki

did. She sucked my Dick till it was rock hard then stood over me. She squatted till she was at the tip of my Dick then played with that clit till she squirted all over me then sat and started riding like she was on a horse.

Kesha got up and stood over my face. I looked up to her rubbing the juices out. I opened my mouth as her water flowed from her pussy like a water fall.

I felt myself about to cum. Kesha seen it. She pulled Dawn off my Dick and they both sucked the soul out of my body.

We kicked it for hours before passing out in the bed. The next morning, they both woke me up with breakfast in bed. "Damn," I said sitting up. "I must of beat it up good!"

"Shut up," Kesha said, punching me in the chest. "I'm about to take Dawn home. I'll be back in a little bit." She leaned over and kissed me. When she moved Dawn leaned in and did the same thing. I gave a cocky laugh as they walked out the room, and I ate my food.

The night before, after Pain and Doe left the club, they hopped in a limo that was waiting to take them home. Moet and Apple hopped in as well. The limo pulled out the parking lot. Moet moved closer to Pain.

"So, Pain," she said. "Who won the bet?"

He looked at her and laughed for a second. "What you mean who won?" He asked looking at her and Apple. "You didn't see Tony and his girl leave together? All Dawn, ma! Hands down!"

She rolled her eyes and said while smiling, "Well, if you had a girl she could be with us too."

He laughed again and replied, "If I had a girl, she would have shot you on site."

Apple looked at Doe and rubbed his tattoos. "I like your laugh," she said as she started kissing his neck. Doe reached over and flipped her on top of him with one hand. "Oh shit!" She screamed as her pussy started jumping.

She moved slowly, rubbing her pussy over the swell of his pants. Doe pulled her dress over her head and threw it on Moet. "What the Hell?" She said looking at Doe. Once she saw what was happening, she went in on Pain.

Doe grabbed Apple's neck as she pulled out his dick. "You so mean," she said rubbing his shit hard. He looked at her hard.

"Violent," he said as he pushed inside her making her scream loudly through the limo.

While Doe was stroking her screams and moans turned into sirens and lights. "What

63

the fuck!" He threw Apple off him. He got back to Goon-Mode. "The fucking cops behind us."

Pain looked at the driver as he put his clothes on. "Yo, what the fuck you do G?" He asked heated as hell.

The driver pulled over. "I didn't do anything." He responded nervously. "What should I do?"

Pain looked at Doe as he sat back in his seat. "What you think G?" Pain asked.

Doe lit a blunt and then laughed. "I ain't high enough for this shit cuz," he said and then hit the blunt. "Fuck it."

The driver turned around and let down the window. An officer approached with his hand on his

DOE

pistol. "License and registration," he said as he flashed his light in the car.

As the driver gave the officer his paperwork, Manny opened the back door to the limo and told Pain and Doe to get out. Pain looked at Doe as he exited the limo. Doe followed. There were two more cops standing at the back of the car. Tracy was sitting in the front seat of the other car.

Anthony Strickland
Killa City

Ki

Ki

"What's up Pig?" Pain said aggressively. "Why the hell you fucking with us?"

Manny looked at the other officers then back to Pain. "We know your boy killed Memphis. Until ya'll understand, we on you. And always got a backup plan."

When he said that, the girls got out the car. They went and stood by Pain and Doe. Moet laughed then went to stand by Manny. Moet kissed Manny long and deep.

Pain instantly got heated. "You Bitches set us up?" He asked with fire in his eyes. He looked at Moet.

She spoke hastily, "Hey, I go for who has the most money." She looked into Manny's eyes.

"You stupid bitch," Doe said shaking his head.

Apple just stood by the car.

"Now look," Manny said. "The Block now belongs to us. We really tired of playing your pussy Oklahoma games boy. Time for ya'll to get that act right ya'll deserve."

Doe got tired of hearing the bitches talk. He pulled out his 45 and shot two of the officers then pointed his gun towards Manny. He pulled the trigger and watch as Manny's lifeless body hit the ground.

"All you bitches get on the ground," Doe said. Tracy, Apple, and Moet all went to the ground. When they were finally on the ground, Doe looked at Pain. "So, what you think? Or should I call Gripp?"

"Shit, it's already two cops dead, fuck it. Kill them bitches."

Doe smiled as he shot Moet in the head. He looked at Apple and she was shaking. He put his gun to his side. He kneeled down and quietly asked, "Why are you trying to set us up?"

She looked Doe in his eyes and answered, "I didn't know anything."

Doe looked at her then looked at Pain. "Yo," he said. "I believe her. I think I'm gonna keep her." He reached down and picked her up off the ground. She hugged him and got in the car.

Pain kneeled down to say something to Tracy. "One thing you out of towners need to learn is that the streets of Oklahoma belong to Gripp and no one and I do mean no one will change that." Tracy looked at Pain and he looked at Doe as well. Pain stood up. "Stand up Tracy." Pain smiled as he stood up. "Yo Doe, kill that bitch."

Doe smiled then shot Tracy in the fucking nose. They watched his soul leave before getting back in the car. "Let's go," Doe said to the driver. He put the car in drive and rode out.

Ki

Yetta and Bam were lying in the bed. Yetta had to pee so she got up and went to the bathroom. She came back and sat on the edge of the bed. Bam sat up and looked at her. "What's up? I know you not still mad about last night."

She turned around with a smile on her face. "Boy, naw," she said laughing. "I'm just not ready to be with a woman."

He laughed and pulled her to the back of the bed. He kissed her long and deep. She got on top of him and started grinding. He reached back and slid her panties to the side and went inside her deep. She moaned and scratched Bam's back. She slowly started throwing that ass in a circle, showing him, she could take all of him.

She put her head by his ear, whispered, "I love you," right before she came all over his dick.

He grabbed her and threw her against the bed and slowly moved in and out of her till she screamed, "Daddy, I'm cumming!" He pushed deeper till she climaxed.

He put his hand over her mouth. She looked at him. "You forget we at Tony's crib?" He asked moving his hand.

Ki

She laughed, "I don't give a fuck," she said cocky as hell. "My brother knows what it is."

He laughed as they got out the bed and went to shower.

The next morning after Kesha got back from dropping off Dawn and Bam, Tasha finally came out the guestroom. I looked at them with a smirk on my face. Bam laughed while Yetta stood there looking embarrassed.

"What you looking at?" She asked with an attitude.

Me and Kesha both laughed loud as hell. "Ya'll nasty asses," I said still laughing.

My phone rang, and I reached to pick it up. It was Pain.

"You watching the news?" He asked as I answered the phone.

"Naw," I said, we just waking up. "What's good?" He then told me about the shit that happened the night before. I'm getting heated the more he talked. "Fuck!" I said as I hung up the phone.

"What's the deal?" Bam asked getting up from the table.

"Turn on the news," I said with attitude in my voice. Kesha ran and did it by hand. When the TV came on, all we seen was *Cops murdered, suspect at large.*

Ki

Bam looked at me. "So, what some cops got killed," he said sitting back down.

I looked at him. "Pain and Doe did that shit." I said getting up.

"What the fuck? How? Damn!" Bam said getting up from the table as well.

They both ran to get dressed and left Kesha and Yetta in the kitchen. "You know it's popping off, right?" Kesha said to Yetta.

"Yeah, I know. I'm going to get dressed," Yetta said getting up from the table.

"OK," Kesha said. "I'm gonna call Gripp."

Det. White called Gripp first thing in the morning. Gripp answered the phone with an attitude, "Why the fuck you calling me so early, Ode?"

"Well, four police officers got killed last night. Honestly, I figured you would be calling me," White said sitting up in his chair.

Gripp opened his eyes but didn't get up. "And why would I call you about that like it had something to do with me?" Gripp asked confusedly.

White laughed. "The fact that I'm the first call you are getting about this might be a good sign. Except the stripper from the shooting is still alive and in surgery as we speak."

"So, what the fuck you saying White?" Gripp asked with an attitude.

White paused before answering. He whispered, "Your son Pain and right-hand Doe did that shit. I have the footage."

Gripp instantly got hot. "Alright," he said as he hung up the phone. He walked to the dresser to get another phone. One thing he hated was not knowing when one of his soldiers made a move without his permission. "I hope he wasn't that stupid," he said to himself. He dialed Doe's number first. Doe answered on the first ring.

"Who this?" Doe asked.

"What? Nigga this Gripp."

When Doe heard that he woke up. "What's good Boss?" He asked in a hurry.

Gripp spoke calmly. "So, you wanna tell me what the fuck happened last night? You know I don't like hearing things from other people before my people."

Doe held the phone as he got out the bed and walked in the other room. He talked for almost 15 minutes. He walked back in the room looking mad as hell. He lit a blunt before he went to get dressed. His phone went off.

Ki

Gripp hung up the phone. "I'm really
tired of the bullshit. When will these niggas
learn?" He asked
himself. He picked up his phone and went to
send a group text. He typed the word *Breed*
and pressed send. He put his phone down and
went to the shower.

I was lying in my bed when my phone
went off. It was a text from Gripp. Glad I was
already dressed. I read the text and instantly got
up. I stepped out the room and shouted "Bam"
from the hallway.

"I'm down here," he yelled from
downstairs.

I ran down stairs, grabbed my keys, and
kissed Kesha as I ran out the door.

Bam took his time and gave Yetta a
long deep kiss before he left and closed the
door behind him.

We both hopped in my truck and headed
to the Pool Hall. Bam looked at me. "Did you
get that text?" He asked.

"Yeah," I said. "I got it. Guess it's time
to go to war."

We got to the pool hall last. When we
walked in, Gripp was walking from behind the
bar with a cup in his hand. He sat at the table. I
guess today was one of those days because

Ki

Gripp looked at Doe and said, "Yo, pass me a blunt." The whole room got quiet.

Gripp hit the blunt and took a deep breath. He spoke calmly. "Now ya'll know these been my streets since I was 10, right? I got these streets because I show love and don't take no losses. No matter who the fuck comes, they need to understand that the streets of Oklahoma belongs to me."

We all listened. Gripp don't usually talk much. You wouldn't even know he was 40 by looking at him. "I'm done playing," he continued. "I figure since they wanna come for mine, fuck it, I'll just take theirs."

Everybody looked at Gripp as he hit the blunt. He continued, "Last night, Pain and Doe killed them stupid ass cops who came with the nigga Memphis. I had Ode make a call this morning and he informed me that nigga Nick sent them after me."

Yella jumped up fast. "Wait," he said as he looked at Gripp. "You mean..." Gripp shook his head. Yella stood still. "When?" He asked pulling out his gun.

Gripp smiled. He knew Yella had been waiting on the green light for Nick. "I know you're ready. Dismissed," Gripp said as he went to the office with Doe following him.

Gripp picked up the phone and called to check on his babies. After hanging up, he

Ki

looked at Doe. "Tell everybody to kill on sight. If I see any nigga of his crew walking the streets, I will kill him myself. Then shoot the captain."

Doe looked at Gripp's face and decided not to argue. He went to the parking lot and gave the order. The war was on.

We all left the pool hall headed to our spots. Bam was still riding with me when we saw Trell walking down the street. Trell had left the squad for Nick a year ago.

When we hit the corner, Yella pulled out his glock. I looked at him and asked him, "In broad daylight G?"

He looked back and smiled. "Gripp said on site," he said seriously. "You remember what happened to the last nigga who didn't follow his orders?"

I nodded as I pulled up to the curb. Soon as stopped, Bam jumped out, and shots rang from everywhere. I grabbed my gun, opened my door, and started letting bullets fly their way. Bullets were still coming as we heard the police getting closer.

I looked at Bam and we both hurriedly jumped in the truck. By the time I put it in drive........"FUCK!!"

Nick jumped out of a yellow Mustang with a Shot gun and started shooting towards

Anthony Strickland
Killa City

Ki

the truck. Me and Yella both ducked as I slammed the truck in reverse. Before I turned around, the tire blew.

"Yella? We gotta move." I said as I opened my door. I got out shooting towards anything moving. All of the sudden, I felt weak. "TONY!" Yella screamed as my body fell to the ground.

"YOU BITCH ASS PUSSIES!" Yella said as he swung open the back door and grabbed the chopper. He didn't even look before pulling the trigger. Nick's whole crew jumped in a SUV and sped off. Yella stopped shooting just in time to see Dana jump in Nick's Mustang. She laughed as she got in.

Yella was screaming as he ran after the car shooting. He finally stopped and ran back to Tony. "Damn! My Nigga just breathe slow." He seen a car passing by, pulled out his Glock and stood in front of it. "GET YA BITCH ASS OUT THE FUCKING CAR!"

The lady didn't hesitate. She got out and ran down the street. Yella picked me up and put me in the back of the lady's minivan and closed the door. He pulled out his phone and texted Gripp as he got in the driver seat and sped away. "FUCK!!" FUCKING HATE MINIVANS.

Ki

Gripp was eating when he got the text. He didn't say a word. He got up, gave Doe a wave, and they both headed out the door. "What's the Deal Cuz?" Doe asked Gripp as they got in the Phantom.

Them Bitches hit us hard and Tony got shot. Yella is in a fucking minivan taking him to OU. "Doe. these frails have pushed the wrong button today. And they fucking around in my city. Plus, you know what this means right?"

Doe looked at his Boss. He knew what was about to go down. Tony's T-Jones was one of the key players in this game before she retired and handed the crown over to Gripp. She felt he put in the right work and now her son is in the ER. "Boss don't trip." Doe said lighting a blunt, "ON THE SET." We gonna handle this shit and Ma Williams."

Gripp looked at Doe. Doe could tell by his eyes that he wanted blood. "Yo Doe." Call Kesha, then text the crew.

"Cool Boss." Doe said pulling out his Note 9. He started dialing as they rode to OU.

Kesha and Yetta were at the nail shop when she received the call. She looked at Yetta and they both ran to the car. While Yetta was putting on her seatbelt she asked, "What's going on? Kesha pulled out her cell phone and sent a text. She put the car in drive and sped down Reno.

Kesha had tears in her eyes driving. She sat her phone down and looked at Yetta.

Worried, Yetta asked. "What is it?"

Tony and Yella were in a gun fight and Tony got hit. Kesha said crying. Yetta didn't say a word as she sat back. They rode in silence all the way to the hospital.

Faba Abba was at the step show watching Beta Theta do they thang when his phone went off. He looked at it. "Kesha? Must be bruh birthday." He unlocked his phone and read the text. His eyes instantly got tight when he seen the message that said Lanell Sky. He stood up and gave a nod to Big Rick and Blake. They all left the gym as he dialed Gripp.

"Yo Big Rick?" Faba said throwing him the keys, "Drive us to Ma Williams G."

Already, Big Rick said unlocking the suburban. Him and Blake got in the front while Faba hopped in the back and put his phone to his ear.

"Faba?" What's good? Gripp said when he answered the phone.

"You tell me." Faba said responding. "I'm hearing bad things going on." "What happened?" "How's my Brother?"

Gripp paused. "I don't know his condition yet, but I will call you when I do. And it's nothing to worry about, we got it handled. Faba took a deep breath. He knew shit was about to get ugly.

"So, who is shooter?" He asked with conviction in his voice.

"Nick and his Crew is all I know right now. I won't know all the details until I get at Yella. We about 10 mins away."

"We on our way there." Faba said as they pulled in the driveway of Ma Williams crib.

"I said we got this." Gripp said with an attitude. We don't …

Faba cut him off. "Nigga I said we coming. See you soon." He said hanging up the phone. "What the fuck that Nigga thinking?" Faba lit a blunt. "Blake, go get Ma."

Blake went in. A few minutes later he stepped out the front door with the Queen. He opened the back door, so she could get in. She hugged her son.

"Hello Robert. To what do I owe this unannounced visit?" She asked. Faba looked in his mom eyes. "Well Ma, got a text from Kesha today." "Shits Bad."

"What did the text say?" She asked looking concerned.

Ki

Faba pulled out his phone and showed
her the text from Kesha. Her eyes instantly got
big when she seen the text.

"Big Rick, Airport." She said putting on
her seatbelt. He nodded and headed towards
Little Rock.

Once they made it to the Airport, Ma
Williams pulled out her phone and called
Kesha. She didn't get an answer. "I will call
once we get to KILLA CITY."

Gripp and Doe made it to OU Medical
first. Doe parked in a handicap spot. They got
out and were met by Detective White.

"Gripp sorry bout this shit. I didn't
know they were in town." White said with his
head down.

"What the fuck you mean? Ain't that
part of the fucking reason I pay your simple-
minded ass? Now one of my captains is fighting
for his life and all you have to say is sorry?

White just stood there. Doe got tired of
looking at him.

"Move ya bitch ass out the damn way."
He said tight. White looked at Doe.

"Who the Fuck You" ...Before he
finished his sentence, Doe punched him in the
face. He fell hard.

Gripp smiled at that then stepped over
White and went inside the ER. Dr. McFadden

came up to him and introduced herself. Gripp
had to catch his self, he had a thing for doctors.
Plus, she wasn't just a 10, she was a 1000.

"So how is Tony" He asked when his
sight cleared.

"Let's have a seat." She said as she
escorted him and Doe to the waiting room.
"Well the bullet went straight through and
didn't hit any major organs. That's a good sign.
We removed the bullet in his leg and another
team is checking for internal bleeding. He
should be in recovery soon."

Gripp looked up and Kesha and Yetta
were walking into the waiting room. Kesha sat
by Gripp. How's my baby? She asked looking
at the Dr.

Gripp grabbed her shoulder, "He gonna
be good."

The doctor got up and begin to walk out
the room then turned to look at Gripp.

"Let me know if you need anything."
She said. He smiled

She turned to leave and bumped into
Yella with blood all over his clothes. Yetta
broke down. Doe went to console her as Yella
pulled up a chair in front of Gripp.

"Yella. Gripp said sitting up. What the
fuck happened?"

Yella looked at Gripp. "Man Boss we
seen that nigga Trell walking the Block so we

got at him. Turns out, it was a set up. Nick whole crew started shooting so we hoped in the truck then a tire blew. As Tony got out the truck, that Bitch Dana shot his ass then ran and jumped in with Nick. I tried to get em Boss.

Gripp held up his hand, "Don't trip Yella, we gonna handle this. Go home and get cleaned up then meet us back here."

Yella sat back. "No disrespect Boss, but I ain't going nowhere until Tony get out of surgery."

"Wait, Kesha cut him off, did you say Dana? Your Bitch Dana?"

Kesha had fire in her eyes waiting on Yella to respond. She knew the answer and quickly jumped out of her seat. Gripp grabbed her arm. She gave him a look but sat back down.

They sat for hours waiting for Tony to get to a room. When he finally did, Kesha and Yetta went in first. While Gripp was waiting, Ma Williams walked in with Big Rick and Blake. She sat next to Gripp.

She started talking. "So Gripp, you having a problem controlling your shit? Why the fuck is my son laying in a hospital? I blessed you with the Crown because I thought you could handle being the king. Was I wrong?"

Ki

Gripp gave her a cold stare but quickly caught his self. He hated being questioned but you don't disrespect Ma Williams.

"Naw, he finally responded, you were on point. You know this game is always about who stronger and I am that one. Like I told Faba, we got this."

"I have known you since you were a kid and even then, you were a cold-blooded murderer, but I know one thing. You better HANDLE this." She pulled out her phone. "I'm gonna leave you Blake and Big Rick. Faba will join you after I'm home." She got up and walked off without another word.

She dialed Tego. He answered on the first ring.

"Ma Williams? To what do I owe this call?" He asked genuinely.

"Hello Tego, she said, shut down the train. No one gets product till the person responsible for shooting my son is dead.

Tego paused for a long second before responding.

"Now Ma, he said, I understand you upset but we got 7 states to feed. Can't afford to just shut down like that. Texas is in town now."

Ma listened to her captain and knew he was right but didn't care. "You heard what I said", She yelled before hanging up. She went in Tony's room.

Tego looked at the phone stunned. He couldn't believe what he had just heard. "Tony? Who would be that stupid to shoot him or try Gripp? Oh Well, YO Curt Blow. Roll up a blunt" then shut the doors.

Blow came in the room. "What the fuck you just say? He asked.

Tego looked at him "I said shut down shop. Apparently, Tony got shot today and it's problems coming." Just then the doorbell rang.

CJ walked in with his right-hand Jerry.

"What's good Tigo." He said shaking hands.

"What's the business CJ? Sorry but shop closed."

"What? CJ said getting out his chair. What the fuck you mean closed?"

"Exactly what the fuck I said nigga." Tigo said pulling out his strap. "Any more questions?" He yelled.

CJ pulled out his nine. "Ain't no questions needed partner," he said cocking his gun.

Jerry tried to sneak Tego and missed. Blow ran and tackled him like they were on a football field. He punched Jerry till his face was smashed then looked at CJ.

Ki

"Yo my bad." CJ said putting up his gun.

"Nigga I don't give a fuck." Tego said shooting CJ in the face. He lit a blunt as CJ body fell to the ground.

"Stupid Ass Bitch." Blow said as he cleaned off his hands. "Im not cleaning this shit up." They both laughed as they smoked.

Doug D was on the block doing his thang when Dana walked up on him in a tight ass skirt.

"What's up Papi? She said slurring that tongue. What's a girl gotta do to have some fun around here?"

Doug D looked at her. "Damn you look familiar. He said. Where I know you from?"

"You don't, she replied rubbing his arms, I just wanna kick it.",

Anthony Strickland
Killa City

Ki

DOUG D

Ki

'Well shit, let's go." Doug D said as he led her to his SUV. They both hopped in the back. "So, what's up? What type of kicking it you trying to do?" He said as he grabbed her titty. She laughed.

"Well let me show you this first." She said reaching for her purse. Doug D was so caught up in her eyes that he didn't see her gun until it was in his face.

"WHAT THE FUCK?" He said pissed. "You done lost your mind? Do you know who the fuck I am?"

She smiled. "Yes, and I don't give a fuck."

She reached to cock her gun when the door flew open. Quove grabbed her and pulled her out of the truck.

"Bitch? are you retarded?" He said taking her gun.

He looked at Doug D. "What's up Boss? Kill her?"

Doug D thought for a sec, "Naw, throw her in the trunk. We will deal with it later." His phone went off. Let's go. Gotta go to the pool hall.

Pain sat at a pool table in his on thoughts. Him and Tony been boys since day one.

Ki

"I'm gonna kill that Bitch wherever I see her." He said taking another shot.

Gripp and Doe walked in. Doe went straight to the bar. While he was pouring a glass, Doug D and Skanes walked in as well.

Pain stood and looked at the door. He didn't recognize the dudes coming in. He pulled out his gun and was about to shoot until Gripp grabbed his hand.

"What the fuck, Gripp?"

Gripp didn't even move. "Chill out Pain, he said, they are Ma Williams people."

Pain set his gun down and took another shot.

Gripp stood. "Everyone shut the fuck up!! Now since this nigga Nick think it's a fucking game, it's bout time we show him just how we play. Pain, I want you and big Rick to head to Crime Bluff and pickup up there. Doug D and Skanes, I want you to find that bitch Dana and bring her to me. Yella. He paused looking at his soldier, go kill Nick.

Doe came from behind the bar and handed Gripp a glass. "Yo, he yelled, I got a new shipment of choppers in, let's get bloody. We ain't taking no more losses. Get the Fuck up and handle the bullshit."

Everyone stood, showed love and left the pool hall.

Anthony Strickland
Killa City

Ki

GRIPP

Ki

"Fuck this," Gripp said grabbing his gun.

Doe stood in front of him. "What the hell you doing with that Gripp?" He said reaching.

"Nigga, Gripp said, I am KILLA CITY!"

He walked pass Doe out of the pool hall. He got in his Chevy and drove away. Doe called Kesha.

Pain and Big Rick had drove half the night. They finally made it to the Bluff.

"Damn, Pain said, I forget to get my damn clothes."

"Chill FOLKS, Big Rick said, I'll take you to go see Roger at Looking Good. Shop, handle business, and get the fuck on down."

"Bet." Pain said turning up the music. HOTTEST IN THE CITY bumping loud thru the streets of Crime Bluff. Big Rick pulled in the parking lot of Looking Good and they got out and stepped inside. Roger, the owner, shaking both of their hands. Pain pulled out a big knot.

"Man here, he said handing the money to Roger. Put ya boy in the Game YA Dig?"

Yeah, Roger said pulling out his best. Pain looked at the fits.

"DAMN Roger, you a matching ass Nigga." Pain said going to the dressing room.

While he was changing, Big Rick seen Mickey and Benny pass by, so he stepped outside to chop it up.

"What's Good G?" Big Rick said showing love.

"Not Shit Cuz, Mickey responded, headed to the Eastside to grab some work."

What you got up my nigga? Benny asked.

"Shit. Big Rick said. MAINTAINING up here with this Nigga Pain about to go see Tego."

What for? Mickey asked interested. You know he closed shop, yesterday right?"

"Man Stop. Maybe for ya'll but Gripp is the King of Oklahoma so his train don't stop." Big Rick said laughing.

Pain stepped out the store in all Polo from head to toe. He walked up and showed love.

"What up EASTSIDE?" He said.

"Chilling Cuz. Heard Nick all in ya'll ass in the KILLA CITY. Ya'll gonna handle that or what?" Benny said looking at Pain.

"Now you know Gripp don't play that shit. Trust we good."

"Aight then. We out. Ya'll be safe." Mickey said.

Ki

They showed love and went their separate ways.

Pain looked at Big Rick, "Let's get to Tego's."

Big Rick Drove towards the Eastside.

Doe woke up the next morning early. He had been thinking all night about how Doug D was acting at the meeting last night. His phone rang. It was Kesha.

"Hello." Doe said when he answered.

"Hey Doe. Kesha said sounding tired. Sorry to call you so early but I need to go home and get some clothes and Tony's Xbox."

"What's good Girl? I'm already up anyway. Give me a hot one and I'll be thru."

"Aight. See you in a bit." Kesha said as she hung up.

Doe got up and walked in his spare room. He looked around at his guns and jerseys. He thought for a second.

"I know I'm gonna kill somebody today. He said to himself. Never shot anyone in my LeBron Laker Jersey." He laughed.

After grabbing a fit and a 357, he went and showered. After getting ready, he stepped outside.

"Damn I gotta stop buying cars." He said laughing. He hopped in the Charger and headed to OU.

Ki

Kesha was already standing outside when Doe pulled up. He got out to open her door. His phone rang as he got back in the car.

"What up Gripp?" He said

"I'm out of pocket today. Gripp said responding. Me and Bee Gonna slide to Tulsa today and take care of some shit. My order still stands."

"No Doubt Cuz. Got You." They hung up.

"What's good Kesha? How you doing? How's my guy?" He drove off.

"Mann Doe, I'm as good as I can be. Just can't believe this shit and the fact that it was that bitch Dana that shot Tony pissed me off even more. I can't wait to see that bitch." She looked evil.

"Yo Kesha, my word, we gonna find all them bitches and lay em' all down. But if I get her, I'll save her for you." He said nudging her shoulder.

She smiled. "Where we going? My house not this way."

"I gotta stop and check on Doug D. He wasn't looking right after the meeting last night. Doe said passing Kesha the blunt. Won't take but a second."

"It's cool," she said as she inhaled, "Damn."

Ki

She sat back as that one hit took effect.
Doe turned up the radio and they grooved,
headed to Doug D spot.

Doug D had a spot on the Southside he
chills in whenever he in town. Nothing fancy,
unless you count the fact he owns the whole
block. He didn't want neighbors, cause
everyone a Suspect.

We pulled to the main house and parked
in the driveway. When we got out we could
here music playing. Loud. A little to loud for
Doug D.

"Kesha? You Strapped?" Doe asked

"Now Doe, im Gripp's daughter, of
course I'm holding." She said pulling a nine out
of her backpack. She cocked it. "What's up?"

"I don't know but keep that 3rd eye open
YA Dig?"

"I got you." She said as they went to the
door. It was cracked. Doe slowly pushed it
open.

"Stay here!" Doe commanded.

"Alright." She said.

Doe stepped in the house. He walked by
the stairs pointing his gun in every direction.

"No One?"

He headed to the living room. He could
see bodies moving around. He pulled out his
phone and turned the camera on.

Ki

He moved to the edge of the kitchen and used the phone to see in the living room.

"FUCK!!" He said as he put the phone back in his pocket. He went back to get Kesha.

"Yo, they got D tied up by the fireplace. I don't know how many and I really don't give a fuck."

"Me either." Kesha said pushing pass Doe. Before Doe could get to the living room, shots started firing. He seen Kesha in the kitchen. When he looked to his left, he could see Trell and Tig running out the door. He raised his 357 and let it loose hitting Trell in the leg and killing Tig. The bullets stopped.

Kesha heard someone trying to reload so she walked into the living room.

"You have got to be fucking kidding me!" She said looking at Dana trying to reload. She pointed her gun at her.

"Get the fuck up!" Dana slowly got up. Walk bitch!" Kesha screamed.

Doe looked up and seen Kesha walking out with her gun on Dana. I see you good girl. He said

"Hell naw, I broke a damn nail. Why you ain't killed that nigga yet?" She asked looking at Trell.

"I was about to call Gripp when you walked outside."

"Call Gripp for what?" She asked

Anthony Strickland
Killa City

Ki

"What you mean Kesha?" Doe said.
"Cause that's the Boss."

Kesha looked at Doe in his eyes as she
pulled back the handle. "And I'm Gripp's
Princess." She shot Dana in the back of the
head. Before her body hit the ground, Kesha
turned her gun and shot Trell 3 times. She
looked at Doe.

"Well Shit, he said putting away his
gun, guess I'll go check on Doug D." He
walked back into the house.

Gripp and Bee were shopping for the
kids at the mall. Hardly ever do they get a
chance to just relax. Bee went to the dressing
room.

While he was waiting on her to come
out, he seen 2 guys watching him. He slowly
moved thru the store and as he thought, they
followed. He pulled out his phone and texted
Bee. He then walked out the store towards the
parking garage. He dropped his bags as he went
threw the door and pulled out his gun.

He hid between 2 cars right by the door.
The two men who were following stepped out
the door. Gripp jumped out with his beam on
one of their heads.

"Why the fuck you following me?" He
said with tight eyes.

Ki

One of the men spoke, "We just going to our car, we don't even know you."

Gripp stood for a second before he heard the gun cock behind his head. He laughed loud. The two men turned and looked at Gripp. One of them walked over and took his gun.

As he did, a silent bullet went thru his skull. Three more shots killed his friend as Gripp did a dip and picked up the guy behind him. He grabbed his neck squeezing the life out of his body. He finally let go when Blake walked up.

Blake kneeled as Mike caught his breath. "Who sent you?" He asked as he reloaded his gun. Mike looked at Gripp and said, "Nick got a bounty on your head. 500 Large.

Gripp laughed. "Is that all. Broke ass nigga's. He reached down and picked Mike up. "You Ok?" He asked smiling.

"I'm good." He said brushing off his clothes.

Anthony Strickland
Killa City

Ki

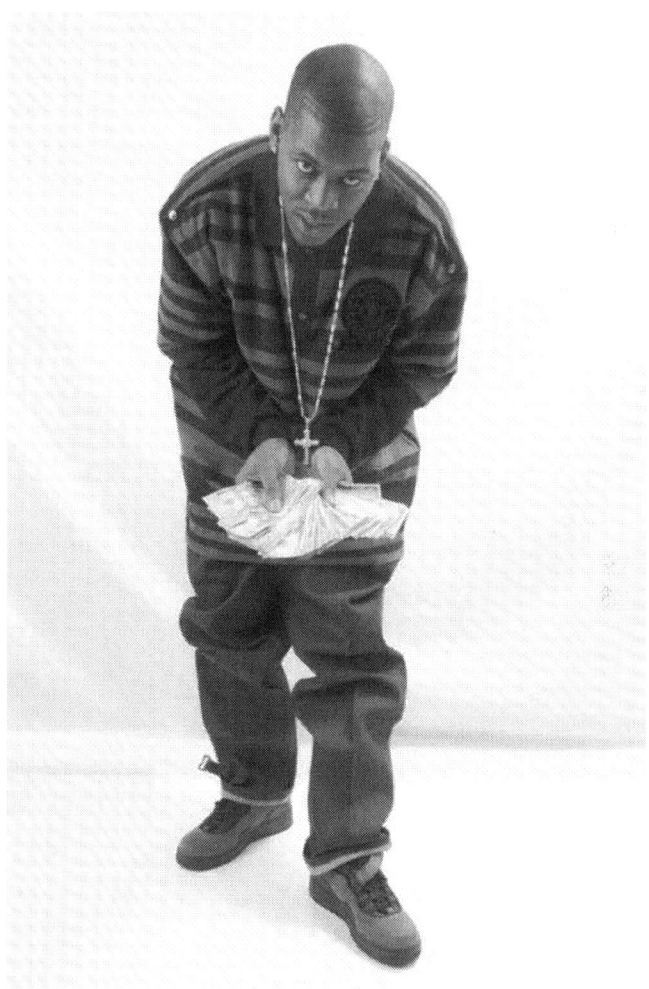

GRIPP

Ki

"Good." Gripp said as he grabbed Mike with one hand and snapped his neck with the other. He dropped his body on the ground.

"Good looking out Blake." Gripp said showing love. They both turned and walked back in the mall.

Bee was eating in the food court when they walked up. "Who is this baby?" She asked Gripp.

This here is Blake. Ma Williams crew. He said grabbing her bags. Let's go. They all left the mall headed to the city.

Nick was sitting at his house in Little Rock watching the news. Shaking his head, he listened

Two body's found on Dixon Rd exit off i40. Identity of the victims being with held pending notification of the families. Police have no suspects at this time. We will update you when we get more information.

He turned off the TV. "How the fuck I keep losing soldiers to this nigga? Time to turn up the heat."

He picked up his phone and dialed Dana.

"Why she ain't answering the phone. Fuck!!" He hung up.

He went to the window and looked at the view from his penthouse.

Ki

"Yeah, I was destined to be King. Time for this nigga to retire. Permanently." He went to his contacts and dialed the Baker Brothers.

"Yeah?" Tim said.

"Got a job for ya'll. Million payout."

"Million? Tim said excited. Who?"

"Gripp. The king of KILLA CITY."

Tim got quiet. He looked at Marcus. "Aight. We got it. Half up front."

Nick smiled. The Baker Brothers always got the job done. "No problem. I will send it over now."

Tim laughed. "GONE." He hung up.

Nick poured a glass of Henny. "I should pat my damn self on the back." He said dancing through the house. "Bout to be the king in this bitch." He sat down and sent a text.

Yetta was sitting with Tony at the hospital when her phone went off.

"Arkansas? What the hell."

She opened the message from Nick. Pissed, she called Gripp.

Gripp and Bee were 30 mins from home when his phone rang.

"Yeah Skanes."

"Got those issues in. We ready" Skanes said coughing.

"Good. I will check in the morning?" As he was hanging up, Yetta was beeping in. "Hey Yetta. He said. What's up."
"We got a problem. She said"
"What's that?" He asked.
"Well…..

NICK

Anthony Strickland
Killa City

Ki

Blacker than Shakespeare's Ink:
Diary of a Nostalgic Kid
by Mr Cordney D. McClain

Paperback
$24⁸⁸

✓prime FREE delivery by Thu, Sep 13

Blacker Than Shakespeare's Ink: The
Diary of a Nostalgic Kid (Grayscale
Version)
by Mr Cordney D. McClain

Paperback
$12⁹⁹

✓prime FREE delivery by Fri, Sep 14

Anthony Strickland
Killa City

Ki

Anthony Strickland
Killa City

Ki

54894722R00057

Made in the USA
Middletown, DE
14 July 2019